Samuel French Acting Edition

I0589028

To Die For

by Caroline Smith

SAMUELFRENCH.COM   SAMUELFRENCH.CO.UK

FOR PRODUCTION ENQUIRIES

UNITED STATES AND CANADA

Info@SamuelFrench.com

1-866-598-8449

UNITED KINGDOM AND EUROPE

Plays@SamuelFrench.co.uk

020-7255-4302

Each title is subject to availability from Samuel French, depending upon country of performance. Please be aware that *TO DIE FOR* may not be licensed by Samuel French in your territory. Professional and amateur producers should contact the nearest Samuel French office or licensing partner to verify availability.

MUSIC USE NOTE

IMPORTANT BILLING AND CREDIT REQUIREMENTS

TO DIE FOR (first edition) premiered at the Lighthouse Festival Theatre in Port Dover, Ontario in July 1994. It was directed by Simon Johnston. The cast was as follows:

CARLA WOODS...................................... Anita LaSelva
GRACE HUNTER .... Rona Waddington
THE MAN ....Richard Bauer

Additional productions at the Muskoka Festival (Gravenhurst, ON), Upper Canada Playhouse (Morrisburg, ON), Baby Grand Theatre (Kingston, ON), Gateway Theatre (Richmond, BC), and Odyssey Productions (Prince Albert, SK).

TO DIE FOR (second edition) premiered at the Stirling Festival Theatre in Stirling, Ontario in 2005. It was directed by Keith Knight. The cast was as follows:

JANET BAILEY ....Madison Kozdas
CARLA WOODS...Kelly Bolt
GRACE HUNTER .... Lora Cotter
THE MAN .... Bradley Garrick

CHARACTERS

Please note: the author heartily encourages color-blind casting.

JANET BAILEY – A brief, non-speaking cameo, which can be played by a production assistant or "junior." A young woman, twenty-something, able to run quickly and appear terrified.

CARLA WOODS – Best-selling author of Gothic romance novels. She is an extremely well-preserved forty-something, striking in appearance, tall, and elegant. She dresses in fantastic gowns, is flawlessly groomed, and always in perfect control of both herself and her surroundings.

GRACE HUNTER – Carla's new secretary and personal assistant. Appears to be a nervous, timid sort of woman in her early thirties. Dresses neatly but inexpensively in business attire. Always carries a shabby briefcase.

THE MAN – Tall and handsome, a perfect "ideal dreamboat" who could have just stepped off the cover of a romance novel. Charismatic and somewhat dangerous; a blend of James Bond, George Clooney, and Heathcliff.

SETTING

A large mansion.

TIME

Contemporary.

PRODUCTION NOTES

Set – Although the unit set appears quite simple, it should be filled with surprises. Many are mentioned in the script: the sliding, full-length portrait that opens, the bar, the corpse in the couch, the stair drop, etc. But feel free to have fun; add a suit of armor that moves on its own, lights that magically swivel, anything to keep the audience on the edge of their seats.

Gunshots – Depending on the resources of the production, these can be theatrical blanks or a sound effect. Local and/or Union regulations regarding firearms onstage must be strictly and carefully followed.

Music – Have fun creating a soundscape for the production. If you don't have someone to create music for your production, there are lots of sound effect and music sites online. Please note: Licensees may not use any copyrighted works in their productions without first acquiring rights. The use of original music is recommended.

Corpse in the couch – The mechanism which activates this can be a simple trigger release worked by Grace as she sits on the couch. The "corpse" can take any form the designer and director find most amusing.

Bar – A very simple effect. The unit is simply pushed forward and pulled backward by a person behind the wall.

Shattering plate – There are several ways to do this. The easiest is to have a line of plates on a plate rail. One plate has been "pre-broken" and lightly taped or spot-glued back together. Attach the breakaway plate to the wall with brackets top and bottom, and a hole behind the center of the plate that a small piece of dowel or metal bolt can be poked through. On cue, someone backstage sharply hits the dowel with a hammer, and the plate will "shatter" and fall.

Broadcast/Podcast – This can be a radio broadcast from a radio or stereo already on the set, or a laptop playing the podcast.

911 – Use the appropriate emergency number for your area.

Stair drop – Most productions have used a trap door at the top of the stair platform, with a foam pad below that the actors can safely fall on. You only need about four feet of height to create this effect. However, set restrictions may result in the use of a fake wall that they can fall through, or any other "surprise" effect. Just make sure the house swallows them!

PROLOGUE

(The time: Today. We are in the dimly-lit main room of a large mansion. The elaborately carved front door sits on a raised platform at upstage center; two steps lead down from this platform into the room itself. Also at upstage is a set of stairs which lead to the unseen second floor. There is a second door in the stage left wall which leads off to another part of the house.)

(The furniture is dark and heavy; strange, discordant music plays. The effect is gloomy, eerie, and "Gothic." The focal point of the room is a full-length portrait of a beautiful woman dressed in a long black gown.)

(There is an offstage scream, and **JANET BAILEY** *rushes down the stairs, obviously panic-stricken. She tries to open the front door, but it will not open. There is a noise from the stairwell, and the young woman looks quickly around the room, then hides in the shadows.)*

*(***CARLA WOODS*** slowly walks down the stairs. She is the woman in the portrait, beautiful in the way that Disney's evil queens are – tall, slim, gorgeous...and deadly. She is dressed in a flowing black gown, and is carrying a small pistol. She smiles like a child at an Easter egg hunt.)*

CARLA. Janet! I know you're down here! Ja...net! Now, where could you be hiding? Here? No, not here. You know I'm going to find you sooner or later, why don't you just be brave and come out now. Come out, come out, wherever you are!

(*Pause...silence.*)

All right, I'll make it more interesting.

(**CARLA** *wears an elaborate bracelet. She presses it, and we hear a loud click.*)

There! I've unlocked all the doors. How fast can you run, Janet? Faster than a speeding bullet? Why don't you try it and see? I'm getting closer! Here I come! I'm getting warmer, aren't I? Warmer and warmer...

(*With a scream,* **JANET** *makes a dash for the front door. Just as she reaches it,* **CARLA** *points her pistol and fires. The shot rings out, and* **JANET** *slowly slides to the floor. Silence.* **CARLA** *walks over to* **JANET** *and nudges her with a foot. No response.*)

You lose.

(*Blackout.*)

ACT ONE

Scene One

(The same room, empty of people. A moment, then there is a loud and hollow knock on the front door, a pause, then another knock. The front door slowly opens, apparently by itself, creaking and groaning all the way.)

(Standing behind it, looking very nervous, is **GRACE HUNTER**. *She is in her early thirties, a bit plain, and dressed in a businesslike fashion. She clutches a briefcase firmly in one hand.* **GRACE** *glances back at the sunny day outside, then looks into the gloomy house. She clears her throat and:)*

GRACE. Hello? Miss Woods? Anybody home?

*(**GRACE** cautiously descends the two stairs from the front door platform and walks to stage center. She looks around the room.)*

Miss Woods? It's Grace Hunter. Your editor sent me?

*(Silence. **GRACE** starts to sit in one of the large chairs when the front door slams shut. She rushes toward it and tries to open it, but it is firmly locked. We hear slow, dragging footsteps coming from above.)*

Miss Woods?

(She starts to climb the stairs leading to the second floor when the lights dim, except for an eerie glow coming from the top of the stairs. We hear demonic laughter, weird music,

and unearthly howls. **GRACE** *backs down the stairs and once again tries the front door, but it still won't open.* **GRACE** *backs across the room until she is standing in front of Carla's portrait. Silently, the portrait slides open, revealing* **CARLA**, *wearing another fabulous black dress and holding a large knife above her head.* **GRACE** *spins, sees* **CARLA**, *screams, and drops to the floor.* **CARLA** *lowers the knife and smiles.)*

CARLA. Welcome to Bridewell House. I'm Carla Woods.

(During the following, **CARLA** *presses buttons on her bracelet. The portrait panel slides back into position, the strange noises stop, and "normal" light comes back on.)*

GRACE. Oh? OH!! Miss Woods! Oh, I feel like such a fool! I mean, your editor warned me that you'd do something scary when I came out here, but I thought he meant that you'd just...jump out from behind a chair or something...

CARLA. I assume you'd like to be my new secretary?

GRACE. Yes. At least, I think so... I'm Grace Hunter.

CARLA. Pleased to meet you, Grace.

GRACE. So far the pleasure's all yours.

*(**CARLA** laughs. **GRACE** opens her briefcase.)*

I brought copies of my resume and references, Miss Woods...

CARLA. Ugh! How disgustingly formal! My name is Carla, and if we are ever to have a successful working relationship, that's what you'll call me.

GRACE. Oh, yes, of course. *(She holds out a slim folder.)* Here you are...Carla.

CARLA. I don't need to see your paperwork. Jack told me all about your preliminary interview, and he recommended your skills most highly. But I don't really care how efficient you are, or how fast you type. If I decide to hire you, it will be because I think you'll...*fit in* here.

>*(CARLA takes the folder and casually tosses it on a table.)*

So let's just chat for a while.

GRACE. Okay.

>*(There is a pause as CARLA studies GRACE, who can't think of anything to say.)*

Sorry, I'm a little nervous.

CARLA. Don't be. If you do end up working for me, you'll soon realize that I am no different than you or anybody else. Except, of course, for the fact that I write best-selling books.

GRACE. And enjoy scaring people to death...

CARLA. Everyone has to have a hobby.

GRACE. Is this house part of your "hobby"?

CARLA. Partially, but it's much more than that. A writer needs to be in a particular frame of mind to create really good work, and this house helps me get there. Atmosphere. The secret is atmosphere. I do my best work when I've almost succeeded in scaring myself to death.

GRACE. But...you write romance novels.

CARLA. Oh, no, my dear, I do NOT write romances, I write *bodice rippers*!

GRACE. Of course.

CARLA. Let's see if you've done your homework. Bodice rippers are...?

GRACE. Also called Gothic romances, and they always have a thread of horror running through them, or some sense of the supernatural.

CARLA. And they generally take place in...?

GRACE. *(Getting it.)* Some kind of haunted castle, or mysterious mansion!

CARLA. Correct! And isn't it marvelous!

GRACE. Yes. It must have some history.

CARLA. You're not from around here, are you.

GRACE. Uh...no. I just moved to the city a couple of months ago. Prior to that, I was working for...

CARLA. This house was built in the 1880s by an English family, the Lyndons. On the surface, the Lyndons were the most respectable of people, but secretly they were amassing a huge fortune by engaging in a rather seedy business – bootlegging. They designed this house like some of the old European castles, with a tunnel running down to the beach – handy for those midnight deliveries – and a maze of secret passageways connecting various rooms.

> (**CARLA** *presses her bracelet; the lights dim, and the portrait wall opens. She lights the candles on a candelabrum as she continues.*)

Of course, as with all mazes, one has to know the way. Local legend has it that one young lad braved the passageways to share a nocturnal tryst with pretty Sally Lyndon, but he took a wrong turn and lost his bearings. His remains were found many weeks later, his handsome physique grotesquely altered after suffering the ravages of rats and mice.

> (**CARLA** *"theatrically" prowls the room, as* **GRACE** *watches her, unblinking, mesmerized by her voice.*)

Can you imagine what it must have been like to be lost inside those narrow passageways? Imagine wandering around in the darkness, turning corners into dead ends, perhaps falling through one of the concealed trap doors – Yes, this house has many dangers. Imagine finding the skeletal remains of other unfortunate creatures who entered before you, your parched throat tightening until you no longer have the strength to scream... *(Beat.)* Let's go!

GRACE. You...want me to follow you in there?

CARLA. You're not afraid of my little funhouse games, are you?

GRACE. No! Maybe a little...

CARLA. *(Blows out the candles and brightens the room lights.)* I'll tell you a secret, Grace Hunter. No matter what happens here – and things *do* happen here – the lights always come back on. *(She smiles.)* Eventually. Even still, I've had a hard time keeping secretaries, a fact I'm sure you're well aware of.

GRACE. No. Should I be?

CARLA. Do you have many friends, Grace?

GRACE. *(Startled.)* Friends? Uh – Well, not... I mean... As I told you, I've only been here a couple of months, I haven't had much chance...

CARLA. No family around?

GRACE. *(Cheerfully.)* Afraid not!

CARLA. No...special someone?

GRACE. No.

CARLA. Ah.

GRACE. Is that important?

CARLA. Not at all. Just information.

GRACE. *(Cautiously.)* You shouldn't be asking those questions, you know.

CARLA. Why not?

GRACE. You must be aware that it's contrary to the Human Rights Code to make inquiries into a potential employee's personal life. Questions like that are essentially...against the law...

CARLA. *(Laughing.)* Against the law! Oh, Grace, don't be ridiculous! We're not "employer and potential employee" here! We're just two potential...*friends*, having a nice chat!

GRACE. But...

CARLA. Besides, I always inquire about friends and family, and I don't give a damn about any ridiculous Human Rights Code. I've found that a secretary who has a very

busy social life has less time to see to my needs, and in
my house, *that* is against the law!

GRACE. I see...

CARLA. Jack informed you of the basic salary, as well as
travel, incentives and bonuses?

GRACE. Yes, it's all incredibly generous...

CARLA. In return, I expect nothing but complete and utter
devotion. Dedication to each task I assign. Loyalty in
all things. You must think of this not as a mere job, but
as your sacred vocation.

GRACE. I understand.

CARLA. So. Do you wish to adhere to some bureaucratic list
of human rights and thereby terminate this discussion?
Or shall we continue?

GRACE. Continue. *(Beat.)* Please.

CARLA. Excellent! Now, as for the dictation of my books. I
keep strange hours, and I expect anyone working for
me to be on call twenty-four hours a day.

GRACE. You wouldn't expect me to live here, would you?

CARLA. Good heavens, no! I couldn't stand having anyone
around me all the time. Then again, I doubt if anyone
would want to be around me all the time. I tend to be
somewhat intense.

GRACE. I think most writers are, aren't they?

CARLA. *(Stiffening.)* I wouldn't know about *most* writers.

GRACE. Of course. Sorry.

CARLA. Have you read any of my books?

GRACE. Oh, yes! All of them! I... I'm quite a fan of yours,
you know. That's why, when I heard you were looking
for a secretary, I just had to apply for the job.

CARLA. Aha! I knew it!

GRACE. What?

CARLA. That's why you're here!

GRACE. Oh?

CARLA. On the outside – a supremely confident, self-reliant
professional!

(**GRACE** *smiles awkwardly. She is none of those things.*)

But inside? – Oh! It's Grace's secret shame! She's just another closet romance junkie!

GRACE. Guilty as charged!

CARLA. I'm very good at uncovering secrets, you know.

GRACE. I can see that...

CARLA. Tell me. How did you become interested in bodice rippers?

GRACE. I guess it was when I was a kid. I'd sneak them from Mom's night table, lock myself in my room and read them for hours. Then I'd dream about handsome knights in shining armor, and that one day I'd grow up to be a beautiful damsel who'd have thrilling adventures, just like all the heroines in the books. How about you?

CARLA. I fell in love with Gothics at an early age too, but I never had the patience to sit and read for very long, so I started writing them instead. While other kids were out wasting time playing hide-and-seek, I was already spinning tales of mystery and romance.

GRACE. How old were you?

CARLA. (*Shrugging.*) Seven, eight.

GRACE. Quite the precocious child! Do you remember any of those early stories?

CARLA. Of course! Want to hear my favorite?

GRACE. Do I want Carla Woods to tell me a story? Uh – yes. Yes, I do.

CARLA. It all begins as Prince Ken is about to marry the beautiful Princess Barbie. But the day before the wedding, the evil Black Knight G.I. Joe kidnaps the princess and drags her up to his horrible castle. Barbie won't let him have what he wants, so he ties her up to his guillotine...

GRACE. Guillotine?!

CARLA. ...And he's about to slice her open when suddenly Prince Ken bursts in! He fights the Black Knight G.I.

Joe off with one hand and unties Princess Barbie with the other! As Barbie looks on in terror, Prince Ken pushes Joe onto the guillotine which falls at that very second and severs his head from his neck! Then, in the most royal of weddings, Ken and Barbie vow undying love and live happily ever after.

GRACE. *(Applauding.)* Wow! You must have been the talk of the neighborhood!

CARLA. Better believe it.

GRACE. So much talent, and so young... What did your parents say?

CARLA. My parents? They didn't even notice. Well, until the day I disrupted my mother's bridge game by holding a séance in my bedroom. Apparently, Mrs. Jeremy Forsythe knocked over a martini pitcher when a couple of kids started screaming.

GRACE. Séances can be pretty scary. Especially for kids...

CARLA. Oh, come on. Kids love to be scared – It's the adults who have a problem with it.

GRACE. What did they do?

CARLA. They tried to make me stop playing my games. God forbid my mother should be the focus of gossip at the club! But I wouldn't stop. Even as a child they couldn't make me...

> (**CARLA** *abruptly stops. She turns and stares at* **GRACE**.)

You clever little puss.

GRACE. Pardon?

CARLA. I believe you just manipulated me.

GRACE. Uh – if I did, it certainly wasn't intentional.

CARLA. Really? Then why all the questions? "How old were you?" "What did your parents say and what did they do?"

GRACE. I told you – I'm a huge Carla Woods fan! I'd like to know everything about you! I mean – as much as you're willing to tell. And I'd never tell! I mean...tell anyone else whatever you tell me. Never! Honestly, Miss Woods... Carla... I didn't mean to pry. Besides, I'm sure your parents changed their minds when you sold your first bodice ripper and showed them the royalty check!

CARLA. They died before that happened. It was an accident. A terrible accident.

GRACE. Oh. God, I'm so sorry.

CARLA. Why should you be? I'm not.

GRACE. Carla, I seem to keep saying the wrong things, and I don't mean to. The last thing in the world I want to do is offend you.

CARLA. Is it really.

GRACE. You just...make me so nervous! Since Jack called me about this interview, I haven't been able to eat or sleep or think about anything else. For the past three days, I've done nothing except re-read your books and wonder about what questions you might ask me. But... I see this isn't going to work out. So, thank you for taking the time to meet with me, Miss Woods. I'm sorry that I...

CARLA. What about my deadline? You know, the one that passed last week?

GRACE. Oh. Right.

CARLA. I'm quite sure that Jack told you – however this meeting went – not to leave without some sort of information about my next book.

GRACE. Yes. I'm to bring him the title, and some idea of the plot.

CARLA. And you, Grace Hunter, are going to make me do that?

GRACE. I really don't believe I could make you do anything you didn't want to.

CARLA. You...are correct. Still. I don't want Jack to have yet another heart attack. So it's time for my story box.

(She takes a small index card box from a cabinet.)

GRACE. Story box?

CARLA. It's where all my books come from. Bodice rippers are all formula, you know. Well-endowed muscular man meets frail young heroine who manages to have her gown torn in all the right places before he rescues her from the evil villain, the end. All we have to do is fill in the specifics. First, an appropriately atmospheric setting. See, in the front – the geography cards. Pick one.

GRACE. *(Selecting a card and reading it.)* "North of Scotland."

CARLA. And the location.

GRACE. *(Another card.)* "Deserted Island."

CARLA. So this story will take place on a deserted island in the north of Scotland.

GRACE. I don't think Scotland has deserted islands.

CARLA. It does now. Next, we have to choose the reason for our heroine to be there.

    (GRACE *continues to select cards through the following.)*

GRACE. "Parents dead, must live with agèd Aunt Augusta."

CARLA. And who the handsome, charismatic but dangerous hero will be.

GRACE. "The rightful lord of the manor."

CARLA. *Very* interesting! The *rightful* lord of the manor! Excellent implications! Now we need some names. Right there, under "Hero First" and "Hero Last."

GRACE. Umm... "Edward...de Villiers."

CARLA. Obviously the heir to a considerable fortune left to him by his French grandfather – if he can prove his birthright!

GRACE. Obviously?

CARLA. And hers?

GRACE. "Christine...Hollingsworth."

CARLA. Christine. Good. Now, add up what you've got so far.

GRACE. *(Reading from the various cards.)* Christine Hollingsworth's parents have died, so she has to go and live with her Aunt Augusta..."

CARLA. Her *agèd* Aunt Augusta...

GRACE. ...Her *agèd* Aunt Augusta – on a deserted island in the north of Scotland where she will meet the rightful lord of the manor, Edward de Villiers! Hey, what do you know – romance in a box!

CARLA. Now, here's where we need just a little skill. To make our story sell, we add lots of adjectives and frill.

GRACE. Frill?

CARLA. Like this. Opening paragraph. "Christine Hollingsworth sighed, turning her lovely face toward the cold, beveled glass of the coach window. The heavy fog did not quite conceal the loneliness of the stark Highland hillside, and Christine's heart wept to think that her dear parents had, that very morning, become part of the earth over which she now traveled."

GRACE. Damn, you're good.

CARLA. Nothing to it. Okay, you pick it up from there.

GRACE. Me? I don't know anything about writing!

CARLA. So? That's never stopped Danielle Steel or Nicholas Sparks.

GRACE. Seriously, I couldn't...

CARLA. Tell how her parents died. First thing that comes to mind.

GRACE. Okay. Uh... "Christine's parents had been hit by a bus."

(CARLA looks at her in disbelief.)

You said the first thing that came to mind!

CARLA. Allow me to expand on that. Buses are neither tragic nor romantic. Try again. And remember to add the frills.

GRACE. Oh, right. "Christine's...*aristocratic* parents had been...*tragically*...run down by a runaway horse..."

CARLA. Make it mysterious!

GRACE. "...A *mysterious* runaway horse...that seemed to come from nowhere!" *(Beat.)* I told you I didn't know anything about writing.

CARLA. And now I believe you. You know, this story actually has possibilities. You brought a recorder?

GRACE. Of course... Jack said you always dictate your stories for later transcription...

> *(**GRACE** digs into her briefcase and gets a recording device.)*

CARLA. And I tend to wander as I create, so you may have to follow me...possibly to places you'd rather not go.

GRACE. Uh... I'm sure I'll manage.

CARLA. I'm sure you will. Anyway, you couldn't do any worse than the last girl I had. She was a huge disappointment.

GRACE. You know, I wanted to ask you about that...

CARLA. Christine has been sent to the north of Scotland to live with her agèd Aunt Augusta in the family's ancestral castle. I'll fill in the setup chapters later. Our heroine, being the young, adventurous filly she is, has quickly become bored in this sterile environment. The only thing she finds interesting in this cold stone edifice is the oil painting of a man. Aunt Augusta has explained – in chapter two, I think – that this man once owned the castle and all its vast lands, but has been dead a hundred years. Christine is fascinated by the painting. She feels instinctively that this man's rugged, handsome face once concealed a dangerous, passionate nature!

GRACE. God, I love it when you write guys like that!

> *(As she speaks, **CARLA** fingers her bracelet. The lights dim, and eerie music plays.)*

CARLA. One stormy afternoon, Christine finds herself in a part of the castle that she has never been in before.

Carrying a burning torch, she daringly descends some slippery stone stairs, clearing thick cobwebs from her face, then ventures down a dank corridor – isn't that a great word, "dank"? – A dank corridor which twists and turns at every step. Finally, Christine realizes, to her horror, that she has stumbled into the family crypt. And she is not alone...

GRACE. *(Whispering.)* Edward!

CARLA. Christine's heart leapt as the tall, powerful figure approached from the shadowy recesses of the vault. She could not see his face, but she sensed that his eyes were piercing through the gloom, eyes which could penetrate her very soul. She wanted to turn and run, but found she could not. As he came ever nearer, the air shimmered with an energy both magnetic and dangerous. Christine feared that, if this man were to touch her, she would be transformed into a single blinding flame which would burn with a white heat, fueled by the passion she had denied for so long.

The torch flared, and for a fleeting instant, Christine could see his face! His dark hair spilled forward onto his brow, but could not quite conceal the scar which told of a lifetime of danger and intrigue. His lips were those of a man who had known love, and had known bitterness. But his eyes! His eyes! Christine found herself drawn helplessly towards those irresistible dark whirlpools! She was drowning, suffocating! She could not breathe, could not move! Then came the stark realization that, despite her fear, she wanted him more than she ever thought a woman could want a man. Drawing a tremulous breath, she whispered,

"Who are you, sir?"

"I am Edward, Earl of Villiers."

"Edward!" she gasps. "No! Edward is these hundred years dead!"

His powerful arms encircled her, and as she drifted down into the silver gray mist of unconsciousness,

Christine's last sensation was the heat of his lips upon her throat.

(**CARLA** *allows the moment to linger, and she smiles as she sees* **GRACE***'s rapturous face.*)

So? What do you think?

(*She takes the recorder from* **GRACE** *and turns it off.*)

GRACE. I think I'm in love! Edward... He's like a wild beast just waiting for the right woman to tame him!

CARLA. And what would you do next if you were Christine?

GRACE. Whatever he wanted...if I were Christine! But since I'm not, there's no way I'd be wearing a flimsy gown and traipsing around a crypt all by myself in the middle of a storm. If that were real life, Edward would have a can of pepper spray in his eyes by now.

CARLA. You mean to say, if Edward showed up on your doorstep one night, you'd just slam the door in his face?

GRACE. Wouldn't you?

CARLA. Absolutely not. I'd invite him right in.

GRACE. A complete stranger. You'd just invite him in.

CARLA. If he was Edward.

GRACE. And how would you *know* that he was Edward?

CARLA. I'd know.

GRACE. Sure you would. Make sure you put me on the invitation list to your funeral.

CARLA. Is there anything you'd like to ask about the job?

GRACE. What? Oh, I'm sorry! Yes! For a while there I forgot that this is actually a job interview!

CARLA. That's fine, Grace. It was nice to see you...*almost* be yourself.

GRACE. Uh... There *is* something I'd like to ask about, if you don't mind.

CARLA. What's that?

GRACE. I'm curious about your last secretary.

CARLA. What about her?

GRACE. Why did she quit?

CARLA. Mostly because she couldn't take my little games.

GRACE. Mostly?

(**CARLA** *looks at her sharply.*)

Sorry, I guess I'm being nosy.

CARLA. No, it's a valid question. If you get the job, what are the pitfalls? By the way, you might also want to know – *where* are the pitfalls!

GRACE. That was going to be my second question. *(Beat.)* You were telling me about your last secretary?

CARLA. Her name was Janet. Janet Bailey. I never liked her very much – She was one of those nervous types. Very good at her work, but overly sensitive, you know? I probably never should have hired her in the first place, but at the time, I needed someone desperately – I was right at the end of *Penelope's Revenge* and Jack was frantic to get it to print. Well, we managed to get through the final chapter when Janet quit and that was that.

GRACE. But what happened...

CARLA. Why don't we discuss all that at another time.

(**CARLA** *puts the recorder back into* **GRACE***'s hand.*)

Right now, I'd like you to take this away and turn it into nice, neat typing. Title it...*The Haunting of Christine.*

GRACE. *The Haunting of Christine...* Wait. Does this mean... I've got the job?

CARLA. You've got the job!

GRACE. Oh! That's... I don't know what to say... Thank you!

CARLA. I'll call Jack and tell him to expect you at his office first thing in the morning, with Christine and Edward in hand.

GRACE. Will you be there?

CARLA. Good heavens, no! What on earth would I do in a publisher's office? Everything I need is here. You are now my link with the outside world and my shield against it. I'll call you when I'm ready to dictate the next chapters, probably sometime tomorrow. Oh, no, I forgot! Tomorrow afternoon, my little tech minions are installing some new toys.

GRACE. Like what?

CARLA. Oh, now, it wouldn't be any fun if I told you, would it? Let's make it Friday. At midnight.

GRACE. Midnight? Uh...couldn't you just...dictate your stories over the phone?

CARLA. No. I need you here in person.

GRACE. Of course.

CARLA. Just remember what I said, Grace. The lights always come back on. Eventually.

GRACE. Can I get that in writing?

CARLA. *(Laughing.)* I think I'll enjoy your company, Grace Hunter.

GRACE. And I think...I'll get used to you in time.

CARLA. Take good care of my Edward.

GRACE. You bet! In fact, I might even take him to bed with me! See you on Friday, then! Goodnight, Carla.

　　　*(**GRACE** exits.)*

CARLA. Goodnight, Gracie!

　　　*(**CARLA** watches for a few moments as **GRACE** drives away, then closes the door. She crosses to the table and picks up the folder containing **GRACE**'s resume and references. She opens the folder and skims through, then snaps it shut, a bemused expression playing across her face.)*

　　　(Blackout.)

Scene Two

(At lights up, the room is again empty of life. A clock may be striking midnight. There are loud knocks on the door, and once again it swings open by itself. This time, however, a real storm is raging outside. A flash of lightning reveals GRACE and her briefcase, huddled under a dripping umbrella. GRACE enters, every nerve and sense prepared for anything. There is a crash of real thunder; she reacts as the front door slams shut. The lights dim.)

(She looks around the room – nothing is presenting itself as a menace. She sits on the couch, and suddenly, a ghastly corpse springs up from under the cushions like a vampire exploding from its coffin. GRACE screams and rapidly backs away. She takes a second or two to recover, then pokes the "corpse" with her folded umbrella. No reaction – It's just a mannequin. GRACE inhales deeply and lets it out in a rush. The game, she thinks, is over.)

GRACE. I like your new toy, Carla. Okay, you got me. Come on out, now.

(The lights snap out. We are now in complete darkness.)

Carla? Carla?

(There is silence for a few moments, then GRACE lights a match. She sees the candelabrum on the table and heads toward it, but the match is burning her fingers and she shakes it out. Blackness. GRACE lights another match and leans over to light the candelabrum, but it is gone. GRACE stares, unsure, then this match also burns down.)

(She lights a third match, and as this one flickers to life it also illuminates **CARLA**, *who is standing behind* **GRACE**, *a jeweled dagger in her hand. Feeling her presence,* **GRACE** *turns around and screams as* **CARLA** *plunges the dagger into her chest. As* **GRACE** *falls to the floor, the match goes out, and we are again in darkness. Beat. Then the lights snap on, revealing* **CARLA** *standing over* **GRACE**, *smiling delightedly.)*

CARLA. Boo!

GRACE. Am I alive?

CARLA. How did you like that?

GRACE. *Like* that??

CARLA. Better than the first one?

GRACE. "Better" isn't the word I'd choose.

CARLA. On a scale of one to ten?

GRACE. *(Slowly getting up.)* Thirteen.

CARLA. Good number. Now, don't be mad, Grace. Look! The lights are back on, just as I promised.

GRACE. Do you have a thing about knives?

CARLA. Not particularly. Why do you ask?

GRACE. They seem to show up a lot around here.

CARLA. Look, it's retractable... This little thing couldn't hurt a fly. But I sure had you going, didn't I?! The look on your face... Would you like a drink?

*(**CARLA** presses a button on her bracelet, and a bar pops out of the wall.)*

GRACE. No, thank you. I think I'd rather get right to work. If you don't mind.

*(**CARLA** returns the bar into the wall as* **GRACE** *pushes the "corpse" back under the sofa cushions.)*

CARLA. Work?

GRACE. Yes. Work. You know, the next chapters of *The Haunting of Christine*? The reason I came all the way out here tonight through the biggest storm of the year?

CARLA. The *best* storm of the year!

> (**CARLA** *crosses to the front door and throws it open. There is a blinding flash of lightning and a crack of thunder.*)

Isn't it wonderful? I can feel that the spirits are with us tonight.

GRACE. *(Crossing to the door and closing it.)* Carla, if there ever were any spirits around here, you'd have scared them off by now.

CARLA. Mmm. You might be right.

GRACE. *(Taking out a manuscript from her briefcase.)* Everything from the last session has been transcribed, if you need it for reference. *(She readies the recorder.)* All right. Ready when you are.

CARLA. Slave driver. Where did we leave off?

GRACE. "Christine's last sensation was the heat of his lips against her throat."

> (*Pause while* **CARLA** *does some pacing and "deep thinking," then:*)

CARLA. I don't think I feel like working right now.

GRACE. Jack said to remind you that your deadline is...

CARLA. I'm so bored, Grace.

GRACE. Bored? You?

CARLA. Yes. Bored by Edward and Christine and the whole romance thing. All I do is tell the same story over and over again. I mean, no matter what I do to them, you don't have the slightest bit of doubt that Edward and Christine are going to live happily ever after, do you?

GRACE. No, but...

CARLA. Then where's the mystery? Where's the challenge? Where's the excitement?

GRACE. The excitement is in the story, in HOW you're going to get them to the happy ending!

CARLA. That's another thing. They always end up the same way, happily ever after, happily ever after... Hey! I know. That's it!

GRACE. What?

CARLA. Let's kill them!

GRACE. What?

CARLA. Let's bump them off.

GRACE. Then it wouldn't be a Gothic, Carla, it would be a Stephen King novel. Look, if you don't feel like working tonight, then I'd really like to head home before this storm gets any worse...

CARLA. Oh, don't go yet. The muse might yet descend upon me.

GRACE. But...

(CARLA *shoots her one of her looks.*)

Oh, all right.

CARLA. You're terribly jumpy tonight, Grace.

GRACE. Wouldn't you be if your boss had just scared you senseless?

CARLA. Are you kidding? I'd be thrilled. I'd love it if something happened in this house, something that I didn't have to create myself.

GRACE. You know what they say, "Be careful what you wish for..."

CARLA. I bought this house partially because of the rumor that there were various ghosts in residence. Well, if there are, they've been on vacation for the last ten years. In all that time – not a single moan. Nothing.

GRACE. I told you. They've had too much competition.

CARLA. (*Laughing.*) Maybe.

GRACE. Carla, I really think I should head back to town...

CARLA. You know what we should do tonight?

GRACE. (*Resigned.*) What.

CARLA. We should have a séance!

GRACE. Oh, you've got to be kidding…

CARLA. My dear Grace, one thing I never do is kid. It's a perfect night for it! Wait here a second…

GRACE. Carla!

> (But **CARLA** has disappeared upstairs. **GRACE** is jumpy and impatient. She paces around the room, looking at her watch, then crosses to the front door. Opening it, she looks out into the storm, which shows no signs of abating. She shuts the door.)

> (Pacing again, she stops at an ornate table, where she casually picks up letter openers, oddities, pieces of mail. She notices a small notebook. Slowly, she picks it up and leafs through the first few pages, her face registering growing shock.)

CARLA. (Re-entering.) Found it!

GRACE. (Quickly tucking the notebook in her pocket.) What?

CARLA. My old Ouija board. For our séance! Maybe we could contact the ghost of that poor young man who got lost in the passageway!

GRACE. Carla, I really have to go. With all this rain, there's going to be some flooding, and I really don't relish the thought of getting stuck in the middle of some dark, deserted back road miles out of town…

CARLA. Then why don't you just stay here tonight?

GRACE. Stay? Here? All night?

CARLA. Sure! Like you said, the roads around here will be pretty bad. Oh, come on! It would be fun! – Like being girls again, having a séance and a sleepover!

GRACE. I recall you saying you wouldn't ever expect me to sleep here…

CARLA. Tonight, I'll make an exception.

GRACE. Thank you, but I'll take a rain check.

(**GRACE** *has gathered her things, and heads for the door.*)

GRACE. Call and let me know when you'd like to...

CARLA. Stop. What's in your pocket, Grace?

GRACE. My pocket?

CARLA. Looks like a small book.

GRACE. Yes. It's a notebook. I always carry one.

CARLA. May I see it?

GRACE. Why?

CARLA. You're acting very strangely, Grace.

GRACE. Am I?

CARLA. Let me see it. Now, please.

(**GRACE** *reluctantly hands her the book.*)

This was Janet Bailey's.

GRACE. Yes.

CARLA. It was on the table.

GRACE. Yes.

CARLA. And you read some of it?

(**GRACE** *does not answer.* **CARLA** *opens the notebook and reads a passage in a flat, bored voice.*)

"Carla is really starting to scare me. I don't know how much more of this I can take. The nightmares are getting worse. She talks all the time about murdering Penelope, but I think she means me. I'm afraid that one of her games will go too far..."

GRACE. She sounds terrified.

CARLA. No, she wasn't. As I told you, she was a terrible secretary – far too sensitive for her own good, and she never did get the hang of playing my games. I found this soon after she quit, and since I didn't have a forwarding address to send it to, I've just held onto it.

(**CARLA** *replaces the little book on the table.*)

GRACE. Of course.

CARLA. And if you wish to continue working for me, please don't go poking around my things. Clear?

GRACE. Yes.

CARLA. Perhaps it *would* be better if you left now.

> (**CARLA** *crosses to the door and opens it. Rain sounds increase. Thunder. Lightning.*)

GRACE. All right.

> (**GRACE** *pauses in the doorway, about to speak, then stops.*)

CARLA. Yes?

GRACE. No. Nothing. Have a good night.

CARLA. I always do.

> (**GRACE** *exits, and* **CARLA** *slams the door. The second it is shut, she erupts in a gale of laughter.*)

Oh, Grace! You are so perfect!

> (*She crosses to the table and picks up the notebook. Where to leave it this time? Aha! She places the notebook in a cabinet drawer, then takes a small key from a cubby hole and locks it.*)

Just perfect...

> (*Suddenly, there is a noise from the front door.* **CARLA** *looks up, surprised, then crosses to the door and opens it. Nothing there but the storm. She laughs and calls out into the dark:*)

You'll have to do better than that, Gracie!

> (**CARLA** *closes the door, glances at the small key in her hand, then looks around the room, thinking. She crosses to a small ledge on the far wall and places the key there. There is a loud knock. Annoyed, she once again opens the front door.*)

CARLA. All right, Grace, enough is enough...

> (CARLA *gasps as a flash of lightning backlights the shadowy figure of a* MAN. *There is a pause, then:*)

MAN. *(With vaguely English "RP" accent.)* Good evening.

CARLA. Hello.

MAN. I'm sorry to bother you, but my car has bogged down in the mud. I wonder if I might use your telephone.

CARLA. Of course. Please come in.

> (*The* MAN *enters. He is wearing a raincoat and fedora, looking like he's just stepped out of an old movie.*)

MAN. Terrible storm, isn't it?

CARLA. Yes.

MAN. I rather like storms.

CARLA. Oh?

MAN. They make my blood run faster. I never know if I'll feel like curling up in front of a warm fire, or tearing off my clothes and running naked through the rain.

> (CARLA *watches him closely. She senses that a game is afoot, but doesn't know what it is yet.*)

CARLA. Really, isn't that fascinating.

MAN. Your telephone?

CARLA. You don't have one?

MAN. You mean a...what do you call them...cellular? No. I'm afraid I have not yet fully embraced the twenty-first century. I dislike most modern conveniences – they tend to interrupt one at the most inconvenient of moments.

CARLA. Yet so handy in an emergency.

MAN. *(With a devastating smile.)* True. I may soon be forced to concede. Meanwhile...?

(**CARLA** *takes a cell phone from a drawer, turns it on, and hands it to him.*)

CARLA. Here you go. Shall I show you how it works...?

MAN. No need. I am not quite a complete Neanderthal... I hate to be the bearer of bad news, but there does not seem to be a signal.

CARLA. Oh? (*She takes the phone from him and checks it.*)

MAN. Perhaps the storm is affecting service?

CARLA. It shouldn't... I've never had this happen before.

MAN. Perhaps someone else in the house has one?

CARLA. No.

MAN. Ah. I take it that you live alone.

(**CARLA** *looks at him, sharply.*)

I'm sorry – I've made you uncomfortable.

CARLA. Not at all.

MAN. Please don't be afraid. If I were a woman, and I came to your door asking for help, would you be nervous?

CARLA. Probably not...

MAN. Then just think of me as...a woman!

CARLA. I don't know if I could do that.

MAN. I'll take that as a compliment. Really, I am quite harmless, I assure you.

CARLA. And just in case you're not, I am far from helpless, let *me* assure *you*.

MAN. Of course. (*A pause, he rubs his hands together.*) It's bitingly cold out there. I wonder if I could perhaps have something to drink?

CARLA. Certainly. Some coffee?

MAN. I'd prefer a brandy, if you have any.

CARLA. A brandy.

MAN. If you have any.

CARLA. All right.

(*Something is definitely going on here.* **CARLA**
presses her bracelet and pops the bar out of the
wall. She pours brandy into a snifter while
continuing to watch the **MAN** *cautiously. He*
removes his fedora and coat, revealing a full-
dress tuxedo.)

MAN. What an interesting house. Fascinating. It seems to –
breathe, almost. Are there any ghosts here?

CARLA. I wish. Why do you ask?

MAN. I have a feeling for these things. I sense that this
house holds many secrets. Perhaps there is a lost spirit
hovering somewhere near us, or a gray specter floating
aimlessly through a...dank fog...

(**CARLA** *starts at the word "dank," but quickly*
recovers.)

CARLA. Here you are.

MAN. Thank you. A toast – to the kind hospitality of the
lady of the house. (*He drinks.*) May I be so bold as to
ask your name?

CARLA. It's Carla. Carla Woods.

MAN. (*Thoughtfully.*) Carla Woods...

CARLA. I see the name means something to you.

MAN. Yes, it does.

CARLA. How nice.

MAN. It means that I now know the name of the most
beautiful woman I have ever seen.

CARLA. Ah. Thank you.

MAN. Carla. So close to the Italian "Cara," dear one.

CARLA. Look, I think I know what you're...

MAN. I *am* making you uncomfortable! I do apologize. I
am overly romantic by nature and it spills out at the
worst times. Please, I meant no offense...

CARLA. None taken.

MAN. Good. Now! A safe topic of conversation... Ah! What
is it that you do, Miss Woods?

CARLA. Why do I feel as though I've landed in the middle of a Noël Coward play?

(The MAN *laughs. A Noël Coward laugh.)*

I'm a writer.

MAN. How marvelous! Fiction?

CARLA. Yes. I write Gothic romance novels.

MAN. Gothic...?

CARLA. Best described as Harlequin meets Frankenstein. You mean to say, you've never heard of me?

MAN. I'm ashamed to say that my knowledge of books is quite limited.

CARLA. Ah – reading! The lost art!

MAN. You misunderstand me. I meant limited to the works of Shakespeare, Lawrence, Maugham, Blake and so on – The great works of literature.

CARLA. Then I'm afraid my poor little books wouldn't appeal to your refined tastes.

MAN. And I am afraid you may be in error. I did mention that I have always been drawn to supernatural matters. And I do have more than a passing interest in the passions which can arise between a man and a woman. You must have a thrilling life to be able to write these stories.

CARLA. Well, I do have a great imagination, and living in this house helps a lot. And you?

MAN. I am what was once called a gentleman. I was left quite a bit of money by my family so I lead a rather unindustrious life. I travel quite a bit, and spend most of my time seeing to my estates...

CARLA. Estates? How many do you have?

MAN. That would be rather vulgar to say, I should think.

CARLA. Of course. My apologies. Just my writer's curiosity getting the better of me.

MAN. *(Leaning in, very close.)* I find your curiosity... charming. Ah! There I go again!

CARLA. We should see if the phone service has returned.

MAN. Yes.

> (**CARLA** *crosses to the cell phone and picks it up. The* **MAN** *silently follows until he is standing behind her, inches away.*)

CARLA. Still nothing...

> (*She turns and gasps to see the* **MAN** *standing so close.*)

MAN. I wanted to see your hair in this light...

> (*He lifts a hand to stroke her hair, and she slaps it away.*)

Forgive me, Miss Woods, I don't usually behave in this manner. I really don't know what has come over me this evening...

CARLA. I would like you to leave. Now.

MAN. Of course. Goodbye, Miss Woods. I am sorry to have inconvenienced you.

> (*He quickly gathers his things and heads for the door. He pauses before opening it and turns to face her.*)

But...if you will allow me a parting word – I have always believed that if I ever met my soulmate, the woman heaven intended for me, I would know her right away. I would know by her smile, by the way her eyes would shine as she looked at me, by the way her hair would gleam in the light. Perhaps I am too much the romantic, but tonight I thought I had met her. I was wrong. Again, my apologies for having disturbed you. Goodbye.

> (**CARLA** *has been listening intently. She smiles.*)

CARLA. Wait! Before you go... You didn't tell me your name.

MAN. Did I not?

CARLA. No.

MAN. How curious.

CARLA. What is it?

MAN. What's in a name? What would you like to call me?

CARLA. I would like to call you by your name. What is it?

MAN. Just a very plain, rather old-fashioned name. Edward.

CARLA. Edward? But – the hero of my current book is named Edward!

MAN. There's proof! Our meeting was destined to be!

CARLA. Perhaps... Perhaps it is possible to fall in love at first sight!

MAN. Perhaps? I say it is a certainty! And if you think it possible that you could love me – even a little – then you would make me the happiest of men!

CARLA. And – are you free, Edward? There are no other women in your life?

EDWARD. None. Although, you should know that I have been married.

CARLA. Oh?

EDWARD. I was very young. So was she. It seems so very long ago now. It was the first night of our honeymoon. We were standing on the deck of the yacht that I had bought her as a wedding present. I turned to pour another glass of champagne, and when I looked back, she was gone. Lost to Neptune's cold, black depths.

CARLA. No!

MAN. We searched, unsleeping, day after day, night after night. But I was never to see my sweet Carlotta again. Finally, I was taken, half-mad with sorrow, to a rest hospital in the south of France. There, I recovered in the ministering hands of the angel who would become my second wife.

CARLA. And...where is she now?

MAN. Shortly after our wedding, we went on safari in Africa. Hundreds of miles from the nearest outpost of civilization, our whole entourage became ill. As nursing was Caralina's gift, she tended to us all through the chills and fever. Just as we were recovering, she herself fell prey. Our happy trek into the uncharted wilderness became my darling's funereal procession.

CARLA. How many wives have you had?

MAN. Seven.

CARLA. And all of them died?

MAN. No, no. Two went insane.

>   (**CARLA** *bursts out laughing.*)

I find it somewhat cruel that you laugh at my misfortune.

CARLA. Oh! Oh! I just can't... This is priceless! Two went insane! Jungle safaris and yachts! Carlotta and Caralina... I couldn't have written it better myself! Oh, this is wonderful! Who put you up to this? I bet it was Jack! That editor of mine always swore he'd get me someday!

MAN. Get you?

CARLA. Or was it one of my legion of ex-secretaries, trying to pay me back for all the games?

MAN. Games?

CARLA. Oh! I bet you have one of those cell phone jammers, and that's why there's no signal. Maybe in your pocket...?

MAN. *(Recoiling from her.)* Madam, control yourself!

CARLA. Well done! I give you an eight. I'd go higher, but you went a little too far when you started in on that gleaming eyes and shining hair bit. You're an actor, right?

MAN. I'm sorry. I don't follow you.

CARLA. Somebody set this whole thing up – hired you for the night to do this little performance! How sweet! Someone does care, after all! Edward. I must admit, you look exactly as I imagined him!

MAN. Do I? That's good.

CARLA. Ah. Now we're getting somewhere. So what's your real name?

MAN. My name IS Edward.

CARLA. Okay, fine. Be Edward. Pleased to meet you. *(She shakes his hand.)* My God, you have cold hands.

MAN. Perhaps I need the warmth of a good woman.

(Suddenly, he kisses her. She breaks away.)

CARLA. All right – too far. The game's over.

MAN. But this is no game. I find myself hopelessly attracted to you, mia bella Carla. You cause strange stirrings in my heart.

CARLA. Lovely. However, I think it's time we called it a night before you get stirrings anywhere else, agreed?

MAN. And therein lies the problem with women today. You imagine the perfect man all your life, then you don't want him when you find him!

CARLA. Listen, Edwa...whatever your name is... I'll be happy to pass on the word that you more than earned your paycheck, but it's been a long day, so...enough!

MAN. I will never have enough of you, my love.

CARLA. This is no longer amusing. I want you to stop this and get out of my house. Now!

(Suddenly, we hear the sound of a deep male voice, laughing.)

MAN. You DO have a ghost!

CARLA. What on earth...? You stay where you are!

*(**CARLA** presses her bracelet several times. The laughter continues.)*

What's wrong with this damned thing?

(The voice begins to chant "Carla... Carla... Carla..." in an eerie whisper.)

Where is this coming from?

MAN. I knew this house was haunted!

CARLA. It is NOT haunted! There is no such thing!

*(She crosses to the portrait panel, opens it, and jiggles a switch on the wall inside. No change. Then an unearthly scream issues forth from the passageway. Startled, and more than a little off-balance, **CARLA** retreats*

> *and just happens to end up in the* **MAN**'s
> *arms.)*

CARLA. Let me go! *(The screams are replaced by strange music.)*

MAN. I cannot ever let you go, my Carla. I will never let you leave me!

CARLA. What is this?

MAN. Everything you've ever dreamed of!

CARLA. *(Breaking away from him.)* This is NOT what I dream of!

MAN. You said you would know me. You said you would recognize your Edward when he came to your door.

CARLA. What?

> *(The* **MAN** *waves his hand, and the noises abruptly stop.* **CARLA** *stands, frozen, staring at the* **MAN**.*)*

MAN. Surrender to your desires. Let me take you in my arms and sweep you into the eternal passion which lies in your soul.

CARLA. Get away from me.

MAN. Will you laugh at me now, Carla Woods? No. You will laugh no more.

> *(***CARLA** *dashes to her desk, yanks open a drawer, and pulls out the small pistol we saw in the Prologue.)*

CARLA. Okay, I'm not fooling around now. This has real bullets in it, and I'm not afraid to use them!

> *(The* **MAN** *is walking toward her.)*

I mean it... Stop!

> *(He keeps coming.)*

Stop!!

> *(***CARLA** *fires. The* **MAN** *drops to the floor. Pause. Cautiously,* **CARLA** *approaches the* **MAN** *and nudges him with her foot. No*

*reaction. She presses a hand to his neck to get
a pulse. The* **MAN** *suddenly grabs her wrist,
and she screams.)*

MAN. They have to be silver.

(The **MAN** *stands, brushes himself off, then
gently takes the pistol out of* **CARLA**'s *hand.)*

You still don't understand, do you. I am Edward. I am
here because you willed me to be here. You created me
out of your loneliness, out of your desire.

CARLA. No! That's not... Just let me think for a second...

MAN. No! Don't think! *Feel!* Trust your heart! Why is it
so hard to believe in miracles when the proof stands
here before you? You have been so lonely, Carla, so
very lonely for so long. But with me, you could find the
perfect happiness that you desire. I can be anything
and everything that you want me to be. Is it so wrong
to want to please you? Is it so wrong for two people to
find love any way they can?

(The **MAN** *passionately kisses the bewildered*
CARLA *again, then lifts her and cradles her
against his chest.)*

Believe in me! Believe in me – and let me love you!

CARLA. *(Whispered.)* Yes...

(Music swells as the **MAN** *kisses her, then
carries her, swooning, up the stairs.)*

(Blackout.)

End of Act One

ACT TWO

(It is early the next morning. There is a knock on the front door. A pause, and then another knock. The front door opens, not by itself this time, but by **GRACE,** *carrying her briefcase and a paper bag from a bagel store. Sunshine floods in from outside.)*

GRACE. Good morning... Hello? Carla? It's Grace, and I've got bagels. *(Beat.)* Do you know that your front door is open?

(No response. Cautiously, she tiptoes across the room, listening for sounds from upstairs. Nothing. Something is worrying **GRACE** *– she stops and thinks for a few seconds. Her eyes light on the small table, and she crosses to it. She quickly riffles through things, looking for the diary where she left it the previous night. Not there. She opens a couple of drawers in the cabinet, then tugs on the locked drawer.)*

(Frustrated, she starts looking for the key. Her rapid search takes her to the center of the room, where she suddenly stops cold, seeing the pistol lying on the small table. She picks it up, when we hear **CARLA***'s voice.)*

CARLA. *(Offstage.)* Edward?

(**CARLA** *enters, floating down the stairs, wearing a filmy black negligee and robe.)*

Grace! Why are you pointing that pistol at me?

GRACE. It was...on the table...

CARLA. Yes, of course it was. What are you doing here?

43

GRACE. Why was this on the table, Carla?

CARLA. The most incredible thing happened last night, Grace...

GRACE. Oh, my God, you actually did it...

CARLA. Did what?

GRACE. Murdered someone.

CARLA. Murdered...? Oh, don't be ridiculous! No, something much more interesting than that. I had a visitor last night. A man!

GRACE. Oh?

CARLA. But not just any man. The perfect man!

GRACE. Who?

CARLA. Edward.

GRACE. Edward who?

CARLA. Edward! You know, de Villiers! From my book!

GRACE. From your book.

CARLA. You don't believe me.

GRACE. I think you're just playing one of your little games.

CARLA. I assure you, Grace, this is no game.

GRACE. All right. Maybe...maybe someone was playing a joke on you.

CARLA. Exactly what I thought. Until I shot him.

GRACE. What?!

CARLA. *(Taking the gun from* **GRACE**.*)* But the bullets had no effect!

GRACE. Maybe you missed.

> *(***CARLA*** *suddenly fires the gun. A plate hanging on the wall shatters and falls.* **GRACE** *screams.)*

CARLA. I only miss when I intend to. No, I shot him all right, and he just walked away from it.

GRACE. He...walked away...

CARLA. Yes! That's when I knew he was really Edward. Then he started saying the most wonderful things, and in the next breath, I was in a daze, in a dream, and my Edward was carrying me upstairs.

GRACE. Upstairs...to your bedroom?

CARLA. Yes. It couldn't have been more perfect if I had written it myself.

GRACE. Well? What happened?

CARLA. I don't know. My last sensation was the heat of his lips against my throat.

GRACE. I don't know what to say... You must have been scared out of your mind!

CARLA. That's the most amazing thing. I wasn't scared at all – quite the opposite. Oh, you should have seen him, Grace. Edward was exactly as I'd always imagined he'd be. Just to die for!

GRACE. How much did you have to drink last night?

CARLA. I didn't have anything... Drink! Yes! Look – his brandy snifter, just where he left it!

GRACE. Sorry, Carla, but a random piece of glassware is not going to convince me that you had some sort of... visitation.

CARLA. You don't believe me, do you.

GRACE. It's just that... It's one thing to write about dream lovers and Gothic heroes and such, but quite another to start thinking they're real!

CARLA. But he was real! A little cold maybe, but real!

GRACE. You have lost your mind.

CARLA. No. I've merely lost my heart.

GRACE. What??

CARLA. Just think for a second – what if all the fairy tales are true, and when two people are meant to be together, then anything is possible?

GRACE. You're starting to believe your own books.

CARLA. But isn't it what we all secretly hope for? That maybe, if we're good or kind or patient enough, we'll be just like all the steadfast romance damsels and live happily ever after.

GRACE. Real life doesn't work like that.

CARLA. Are you sure? Women don't dream about the realities of relationships – What woman swoons over the drudgery of washing sweaty socks? Or balancing an overdrawn checking account or scrubbing a toilet? Romance novels and sexy vampire movies and reality-TV dating shows are multi-billion dollar industries for one very good reason – they help us hang on to the dream that those fantastic things just might happen to us. Well, Grace, it finally happened to me.

GRACE. I'm…having trouble believing that this isn't just some new game you're playing…

CARLA. I have absolutely no interest in what you may or may not believe. I know what happened last night, and that's enough for me. Anyway, you might as well go home now. I'm not in the mood to work today. I think I'll change into something to dream in and then spend the rest of the day doing exactly that.

> (**CARLA** *heads toward the stairs then stops, turning to* **GRACE** *with a sweet smile.*)

Maybe someday the magic will happen for you, Grace. Then you'll understand.

> (**CARLA** *heads upstairs.* **GRACE** *looks after her for a few seconds, in total bewilderment. She picks up some of the shattered pieces of plate, looks at the bullet hole in the wall. As her back is turned, the portrait panel slowly opens, and the* **MAN** *emerges, in rumpled shirt sleeves, rather cobwebby. He tiptoes across the room and suddenly grabs* **GRACE**, *covering her mouth with his hand. Surprised, she yelps.*)

MAN. Sssshhhh!

CARLA. *(From upstairs.)* Grace? Did you say something?

MAN. Say no.

> (*The* **MAN** *uncovers her mouth long enough for her to say:*)

GRACE. No!

CARLA. I told you, you might as well go home. So go home!

MAN. Say all right.

GRACE. All right!

> *(The* **MAN** *takes his hand away from* **GRACE**'s *mouth, indicating that she is to remain silent. He crosses to the front door, opens it, and closes it with a slam. The* **MAN** *listens for a moment – no sound from upstairs.)*

MAN. She's in her bedroom. We're alone.

GRACE. *(Suddenly smacking him on the shoulder.)* I am so furious with you!

MAN. Why? I did everything you told me to!

GRACE. You also did a few things of your own by the sound of it. I've been going out of my mind! Why didn't you call me?

MAN. I couldn't – I've been in that passageway all night.

GRACE. What?

MAN. Thank God I heard the two of you talking just now, otherwise, I'd still be... *(He shudders.)* It's a long story.

GRACE. Did I not make it clear that you were to show up last night for one hour – *one hour!* – scare the hell out of her, then leave?

MAN. You did.

GRACE. She says she shot you...

MAN. She did.

GRACE. And you took her upstairs!

MAN. I did.

GRACE. So did you also...

MAN. I didn't! What kind of a man do you think I am?

GRACE. I think I'm just beginning to find that out!

MAN. Hey! You're the one who set this whole thing up! I'm just the hired help, who, by the way, pulled off the best improvisational work of his career last night.

GRACE. Oh, like that's saying a lot.

MAN. Excuse me? You have no reason to criticize my "method," babe! Carla was so convinced that I really was Edward, she's half in love with me already!

GRACE. She wasn't supposed to fall in love with you, you jerk, she was supposed to be terrified of you.

MAN. Can I help it if I'm...irresistible?

GRACE. Oh, spare me! Maybe it would have been better if Carla had actually shot you.

MAN. Ah, but thanks to your generous bribes, the special effects guys switched the bullets for blanks, didn't they.

GRACE. Apparently not completely. Carla just turned a plate into dust with one of those blanks.

MAN. What?! *(He grabs the pistol and looks inside.)*

GRACE. For a while there I thought you were probably garden fertilizer by now.

MAN. Damn! They must have only loaded one blank – the rest of the bullets in here are real! One more shot last night and that dust would have been me!

GRACE. Irresistible – and dead!

MAN. That's not funny. Okay. This performance is now over. I'm outta here.

GRACE. I'll call you later and you can fill me in on *all* the details.

MAN. Okay.

GRACE. Make sure you return the tux.

MAN. Yeah, yeah...

GRACE. And the devices?

MAN. Oh, yeah. I almost forgot. Remote control...phone jammer.

(He hands them to **GRACE.***)*

Carla almost found them in my pocket last night... That was a tense moment, I can tell you...

GRACE. You took out the extra speakers?

MAN. Nope. *(Pointing to the passageway.)* They're still in there.

GRACE. Idiot! You were supposed to take everything out!

MAN. That's what I was trying to tell you! The cables run way back into the passageway. I disconnected them, then got totally lost trying to find my way back, which is why I'm still here!

GRACE. Oh, come on...

MAN. Have you been in there?

GRACE. No.

MAN. Try it sometime. You'll see.

GRACE. Look, my deal with Carla's effects guys was that all the extras they put in for us would be gone before Carla had a chance to figure out what happened...

MAN. Okay, okay. I'll do it now. But if I'm not back in three minutes, send a search party.

GRACE. Oh, and listen – if you find a key in there, I want it.

MAN. A key?

GRACE. Yeah. Probably fairly small. It opens one of those drawers.

MAN. No way. I'm not going to be an accessory to...whatever it is you're planning now.

GRACE. Nothing illegal. But I need that key.

MAN. Maybe Carla has it with her.

GRACE. Oh, no. It's right here somewhere. She wants me to find it.

MAN. How do you know that?

GRACE. Because I know her. This is one of her little games.

MAN. What?

GRACE. Just hurry and get those speakers out – we've already wasted too much time!

> *(The* **MAN** *disappears into the passageway.* **GRACE** *looks around the room. She sees the little ledge, dashes to it, and finds the key. Before* **GRACE** *can open the drawer, the* **MAN** *emerges from the passageway, holding a woman's purse.)*

MAN. I didn't find a key...

GRACE. That's okay, I've found it.

MAN. ...But I did find this.

GRACE. *(Looking through the purse.)* Wallet...ID, all belonging to Janet Bailey.

CARLA. *(From upstairs.)* Grace?

> *(The door upstairs slams. Realizing that* **CARLA** *is on her way down, the* **MAN** *grabs the purse from* **GRACE** *and heads for the secret panel, closing it behind him.* **GRACE** *slips the key into her pocket as* **CARLA** *enters, wearing a slinky "day dress.")*

Grace! I thought you left.

GRACE. *(Thinking quickly.)* I did...but I came back because I felt sorry about telling you that I didn't believe in Edward and everything. So I thought maybe you and I could have breakfast and talk about it some more. *(She picks up the bagel bag.)* I brought bagels...

CARLA. I'm not much of a breakfast person.

GRACE. Well, how about some coffee, then? Come into the kitchen and I'll have it going in a second.

CARLA. No, thanks.

GRACE. If you don't like bagels, I make the world's best waffles...

CARLA. No, thanks.

GRACE. Light, fluffy pancakes...

> *(***CARLA** *simply stares daggers at her.)*

I'm simply concerned about you, Carla. I mean, you seem to have had some sort of...experience...last night, and...

CARLA. Uh-huh. Last night you couldn't wait to leave, now you want to stay. What a strange person you are, Grace Hunter. Unless, of course, there's something you want here, something you want very much.

> *(***CARLA** *glides to the little shelf and runs her hand along it – no key, of course.)*

Being nosy can get you in a lot of trouble.

GRACE. So can reading other people's private journals.

CARLA. Perhaps.

GRACE. Why did you keep it?

CARLA. Why are you so interested in Janet Bailey?

GRACE. I have my reasons.

CARLA. You know what happened to her, don't you.

GRACE. Yes. But I wanted proof.

CARLA. Her journal?

GRACE. And her purse.

CARLA. You *have* been busy!

GRACE. I'll ask you again. Why did you keep her things?

CARLA. Why shouldn't I? I have nothing to hide.

GRACE. What??

CARLA. Unless, of course, you go stirring things up. And since I have a feeling that's exactly what you intend to do, you leave me no choice...

(They both dart for the pistol, but **CARLA** *easily grabs it first.)*

Now, I wonder what you would do if this gun was in your hand, Grace? I wonder if you'd actually be able to use it. You know, It takes a special kind of person to commit a murder, and I don't think you're that kind of person. I, on the other hand...

*(***CARLA*** *points the pistol at* **GRACE***, who is silent.)*

Nothing to say for yourself, Gracie? No pleading, no begging? Come on, I'll help you get in the mood. Chapter Three... "Christine awoke to find herself at the mercy of her captor, who stood over her with pistol cocked and ready to fire..." Oh, interesting double entendre there, I must remember that...

GRACE. Is this what you did to Janet?

CARLA. Wouldn't you like to know.

GRACE. Yes, I really would.

CARLA. I'd like it if you were a little more scared, Gracie...

GRACE. Scared of you? And your stupid games? I don't think so.

CARLA. But this time, I'm not playing a game. I'm very serious. I can't have you running around telling all sorts of lies about me.

GRACE. They wouldn't be lies, Carla. I would tell the truth.

CARLA. There's an old proverb, my dear – Only children and fools speak the truth. Goodbye, Gracie, it's been fun...

> (CARLA *begins to pull the trigger. Suddenly, the portrait panel flies open to reveal the* MAN, *once again in full tuxedo.)*

Edward!

MAN. Dearest! I had to see your lovely face once more before I leave you for all eternity!

CARLA. You ARE real! You've come back! Oh, Edward!

> (CARLA *throws her arms around his neck, kissing him passionately.* GRACE *realizes that the* MAN *is deliberately distracting* CARLA, *so she starts to head toward the door.)*

I thought I'd imagined you! I was beginning to think that last night never happened at all, but it's day and you're here! Oh, Edward!

MAN. You are the reason for my being!

CARLA. My soul's desire!

MAN. How I have longed to taste these lips again!

CARLA. Then taste them, my love, for they are yours forever!

> (They kiss again. GRACE *is just about to open the front door.* CARLA *suddenly breaks free of the* MAN, *pointing the pistol at* GRACE.)

Don't you move another step.

MAN. (*Madly improvising.*) Who...who is this...fair maiden, my love?

CARLA. This is no fair maiden, dear heart, but an evil witch who has come to steal our happiness.

MAN. Our happiness cannot be stolen, my sweet. It is locked away in the fortress of my heart!

CARLA. She has threatened me with her wicked lies!

MAN. Lies too cannot touch us! We are beyond the reach of such poisons! I am certain the maid has not done you a great wrong. Can you not find forgiveness in your heart?

CARLA. No! Let us dispatch this tormentor, Edward! We will send her back to hell!

MAN. This I cannot allow, my sweetest lady...

CARLA. You dare refuse my request?

MAN. I must!

CARLA. Then you do not love me!

> (**CARLA** *aims at the* **MAN** *and pulls the trigger.* **GRACE** *screams as the* **MAN** *reels back, his hands clutching at his chest. He stands, swaying for a few seconds, then takes a red-stained hand away from his chest, showing his white shirt-front soaked with blood. He crumples to the floor and lies still.*)

GRACE. Oh my God... OH MY GOD!!

CARLA. Congratulations, my dear. I award this game to you.

GRACE. What...?

CARLA. You're the first person who has actually managed to give me a run for my money.

> (**GRACE** *is staring at her.*)

Oh, yes, I know all about the two of you, and your little scheme.

GRACE. All right, but...but you didn't have to kill a man in cold blood!

CARLA. His blood was pretty hot, if you ask me.

GRACE. How can you...

CARLA. How can I? How could *you*. You tried to make a fool of me, and I can never allow that.

> (**CARLA** *once again levels the gun at* **GRACE**.)

GRACE. You'll never get away with it.

CARLA. Oh, what a dreadful line! Can't you come up with something a little more original?

GRACE. But you won't get away with it.

CARLA. You don't think so? You forget how good I am with dialogue. "Oh, Officer! This lunatic – a crazed fan, I think – followed my secretary into the house this morning and found the pistol I keep in my desk and...shot her. Then he tried to attack me! Oh, it was horrible! Somehow, I managed to keep my wits about me, and I sweet-talked him into putting the gun down. Then, when he was distracted, I grabbed it and... Oh! I can't go on... Poor darling Grace!" There! Isn't that a good story?

GRACE. A story full of holes...

CARLA. Oh, darling, you're so naïve! The world simply loves celebrities, and when you're rich and famous, you can get away with all sorts of nasty things, even murder. You know, I doubt the world will notice the loss of another bad actor. Or, for that matter, another bad secretary. Still believe I'm just playing games, Grace?

    (**GRACE** *is silent.*)

Chapter Twelve. "Christine now faced the evil vixen who had tormented her life, and steeled herself for the task she knew was inevitable."

GRACE. Carla, stop it.

CARLA. "Her soft, white hand trembled gently as she raised the jeweled hilt of the lover's pistol..."

GRACE. No...

    (**GRACE** *screams as the* **MAN** *springs up from the ground and grabs* **CARLA**'s *arm as the pistol fires. Their struggle becomes a passionate embrace, then* **CARLA** *and the* **MAN** *begin to giggle. They look at* **GRACE**, *who is staring at them, and the giggles turn into howls of laughter.*)

CARLA. Grace! You should see your face!

MAN. Now, THAT was the best improv I've ever done! Man, am I good or what?!

CARLA. Truly inspired, my dear – bravo!

GRACE. A game. This whole day has been a game.

MAN. Uh-oh, I think Grace is a little upset with us.

CARLA. Why should she be? I'm the only one who has the right to be angry.

GRACE. So what did happen here last night?

CARLA. Well, you know most of it. He was carrying me upstairs, and I was playing dead...

MAN. Playing dead? You were swooning with passion!

CARLA. Oh, please! I was acting!

MAN. Yeah, right. Anyway, after I put her onto her bed, I went into the passageway to take out our effects, all according to plan. Jeez, it's creepy in there! Next thing I know, Carla is suddenly standing right in front of me.

CARLA. I didn't realize that a man could scream quite that loud.

MAN. So there I was, caught red-handed...

CARLA. He confessed. Told me everything about your clever little scheme to make me believe that Edward had come to life. Then I got an idea.

MAN. We could turn the tables on you. Even stage my "death"!

CARLA. It was perfect!

MAN. Oh, come on, Grace. Where's your sense of humor?

CARLA. Grace doesn't appreciate a good joke like you do, my dear.

GRACE. *(To* **CARLA.***)* And was Janet also a joke to you?

MAN. *(Wearily –* **GRACE** *is spoiling his mood.)* Oh, not the trials of Janet again.

GRACE. What do you know about it?

MAN. Carla told me everything. Janet worked here. One night she freaked out. She quit. So what? People quit jobs every day.

GRACE. Did Carla tell you that Janet Bailey is dead?

MAN. *(Uncomfortable.)* Well – yeah. She committed suicide.

GRACE. Because Carla made her life miserable.

CARLA. Her life was already miserable.

GRACE. Thanks to your sick little games.

MAN. What's going on here?

GRACE. Why don't we tell him the truth, Carla?

CARLA. Go ahead. I'd like to hear your version of it.

GRACE. Janet was my closest friend. I remember the day she landed this job, I had never seen her so happy! She was going to be working with her favorite author, the fabulous Carla Woods! Did you know how much she idolized you, trusted you? How stupid of me – of course you did. Her trust made her easy prey. You lost no time in starting to play your games with her, and the more neurotic she became, the more fun she was to scare, isn't that right? Then one night you shot her.

CARLA. *(Bored.)* It was just a game of hide and seek, and they were blanks.

GRACE. You made her believe they were real, something you do very well.

CARLA. Janet passed out by the front door for a few seconds, then she came to and went home.

GRACE. But what was her state of mind when she left for home? She was hysterical, wasn't she.

CARLA. No.

GRACE. She called me that night, drunk and incoherent. I could barely understand what she was saying. Her neighbor called 911, said there was a woman screaming in the next apartment. The police got there in time to see her jump, and I arrived a few minutes later. Ever seen the body of someone you care for after they've fallen twenty floors, Carla? It's not what you'd call a romantic death.

CARLA. And you think I am responsible.

GRACE. I know you are.

CARLA. *(Shrugs.)* If Janet had ever mentioned that my games were causing her distress, I would have stopped.

GRACE. No. You wouldn't have. You're a thrill junkie, and every thrill has to be bigger than the one before. Janet's journal proves...

CARLA. Proves nothing! Somebody always has to take the blame, don't they! There are no accidents anymore, just lawsuits waiting to be tried! Well, sometimes things just happen, and they're called tragedies, and we all feel very sad for a while, then we get over it. So get over it.

GRACE. You're a monster, Carla Woods.

> *(There is a brief pause as* **CARLA** *and* **GRACE** *glare at each other. Then* **CARLA** *smiles and turns to the* **MAN**.*)*

CARLA. My dear, I think you should go now.

MAN. So soon? Things are just starting to get interesting.

CARLA. You need to get into a shower and some clean clothes.

MAN. Well, maybe you're right. This fake blood is starting to drip into my shorts.

CARLA. I really had fun last night. Want to do it again some time?

MAN. Uh... *(Glancing at* **GRACE**, *who glares back at him.)* I think...

CARLA. We have a lot to discuss. You know, we're about to turn a couple of my books into films, and I have casting approval.

MAN. Really?

CARLA. You were so convincing as Edward. I think you should continue playing him.

MAN. *(As Edward.)* That would be my greatest pleasure, my lady!

CARLA. Here is my private number. I guarantee it won't be jammed. Call me and we'll set up a meeting.

MAN. Count on it.

(**CARLA** *opens the front door for him. He pauses.*)

MAN. Bye Grace.

(*But* **GRACE** *is silent.*)

Bye Carla.

CARLA. See you around, dream man.

(*With a wink and a smile, he exits.* **CARLA** *closes the door behind him.*)

GRACE. You are some piece of work.

CARLA. Thank you. Nice to be appreciated.

GRACE. What sort of games are you going to play with him?

CARLA. Oh, I don't know. Maybe I'll make him my next secretary.

GRACE. A male secretary? I thought you only liked timid women who scare easily.

CARLA. What is it that you want from me, exactly?

GRACE. Among other things, I want you to admit that you are responsible for Janet's death.

CARLA. That subject is becoming tiresome. Let's talk about that tenacious girl journalist, Grace...Bennett.

GRACE. (*Taken aback.*) How long have you known that?

CARLA. Oh, instant admission of guilt! Boring, boring, boring!! Come on, Grace, deny it! Tell me a story!

GRACE. That's your game. Carla, not mine. If you knew about me, why did you hire me?

CARLA. I didn't know at first. But I checked out that fake resume, like those incompetent idiots at my office should have. Grace "Hunter"? I know a pseudonym when I hear it. Seriously, you should have selected something a little less obvious. It didn't take me long to find Grace Bennett, investigative reporter – I didn't know that career still existed! Very impressive. Anyway, I hired you because I thought it would be fun to find out what you really wanted, and to see how long you could keep up the facade of timid, mousy Grace Hunter.

A word of advice – If you're thinking of becoming an actress, don't give up your day job.

GRACE. Thanks.

CARLA. What I missed of course, was the relationship between you and Janet Bailey. I must be slipping in my old age. So. What are you going to do now, Girl Journalist? Write a blog? Or a feature? A fascinating in-depth article about how naughty Carla Woods can be?

GRACE. I am going to have so much fun writing it. I am going to...

CARLA. What? Describe me as a monster? Create a scandal that will be the end of my writing career? *(She laughs.)* Oh, my dear Grace, you truly have no idea how the world works! Go ahead and write anything you like about me! You know what will happen? Sales of my books will skyrocket! Jack won't be able to handle all the offers of book tours, lectures and talk shows! It'll finally push Brangelina *[or whatever story is on current tabloid covers]* off the front pages of the tabloids! Oh, please write your article, Grace, please, oh please!

GRACE. You're missing the obvious.

CARLA. Am I?

GRACE. I'm going to tell them about last night. I'm going to tell them that Carla Woods leads such a pitiful and lonely life that one dark and stormy night, she actually believed that a character from one of her books had come to life.

CARLA. I never for a second believed...

GRACE. Oh, yes, you did! For a few precious seconds last night, you fell for it. You *believed*. That's really burning you up, isn't it.

CARLA. Don't be ridiculous.

GRACE. Tell me Carla – how did it feel when you discovered that the man of your dreams was just some out-of-work actor? What came first? – The hurt? Or the fury when you realized that somebody had outmaneuvered you at your own game?

CARLA. Do go on – I'm fascinated.

GRACE. Well, playtime is finally over. By writing the truth about you, I'm going to take away your games. Oh, not the scary noises and mysterious passageways and such – You can keep those. I mean your nasty little mind games. I'm going to let everyone into your head, and after that, no-one will ever come here again without knowing exactly what's going to happen. I imagine Jack will lose his job – he's obviously been enabling your sadistic little habits for years. Oh, the lengths people go to, to keep the cash flowing in! Anyway, the important thing is – you will never get to torture another Janet Bailey. Ever. You'll have no more carefully chosen nervous secretaries, no more entourage to tease. *You will have nobody left to play with.* What will life be like for you then, Carla Woods?

CARLA. I'll manage.

GRACE. Will you? Hey, Miss Woods – tell me again how your parents died.

CARLA. It was an accident. A terrible accident.

GRACE. Car accident? House fire? Plane crash?

(**CARLA** *is silent.*)

You've been telling that sad tale for so many years now, I think you believe it yourself. But the truth is that your parents are alive and well – I spoke to them a few days ago. They didn't know that you get a kick out of telling people they're dead.

CARLA. How dare you...

GRACE. Come on, Carla, I know your secrets. All of them. Why don't you concede that you played *my* game, and lost.

CARLA. I never lose.

GRACE. But I've beaten you, haven't I! I set up a trap, and you fell right into it.

CARLA. I never lose.

GRACE. You're no different than any other lonely, desperate, wrong-side-of-forty woman, which you'll realize when I shine a light on your private little empire. No more total control, no more power. Game, set, match, you lose!

CARLA. *I NEVER LOSE!!*

GRACE. There she is. There's the real Carla Woods. Still that creepy little girl who only feels alive when she's holding séances in her bedroom.

CARLA. Get out of my house...

GRACE. Why? Don't you like *my* scary games, Carla?

CARLA. I...have apparently...underestimated you.

GRACE. No. You just overestimated yourself.

> (**GRACE** *takes the key from her pocket, opens the drawer, and removes the journal.*)

And if anyone needs more proof, all they have to do is read this.

CARLA. Don't do this. I'm warning you.

GRACE. Is that panic I hear in your voice? Are you actually frightened? Not a very nice feeling, is it?

> (**GRACE** *gets Janet's purse from the passageway.*)

CARLA. I'll stop. I promise I won't play any more games.

GRACE. That's right. You won't.

> (**GRACE** *heads for the front door.*)

CARLA. Stop!!

> (**CARLA** *has grabbed the pistol and is aiming it at* **GRACE**.)

GRACE. So predictable. When in doubt, begin another game. Well, we're playing by my rules now, and I say it's game over.

> (*As* **GRACE** *turns to the door,* **CARLA** *fires a single shot.* **GRACE** *spins round to face* **CARLA**,

dropping her briefcase as her hand goes to her back. As she slowly slides to the floor, she brings her hand forward – It is covered in blood.)

CARLA. *Now* it's game over.

(With a bang, the portrait wall slams open, revealing the MAN.)

MAN. Not quite.

(Blackout.)

EPILOGUE

*(Still in blackout, we hear the **MAN**'s voice reading the following.)*

VOICE-OVER. "Christine leapt onto the broad, powerful back of Edward's faithful horse, Ebony. The storm blew her velvet cape around her lithe body as she urged the beast forward with her rain-moistened thighs.

"The stallion thundered across the moor, his jet mane streaming behind him like the wind. And there! There was her Edward, lying where the villainous Count Vladimir had left him, his lifeblood seeping into the earth like the tears of fallen angels. Ebony reared mightily and shuddered to a halt. Christine felt her tender young heart break as she ran toward the lifeless body of the only man she had ever loved. She threw herself on the hard, cold ground beside him and held the firm, warm body close to her, so close that she soon found herself lying full-length upon his hard, muscular chest, kissing those dear lips again and again.

> *(The lights come up, revealing the **MAN** listening to a podcast. He is dressed casually, in jeans and a sweater, and is smiling, getting a kick out of what he is hearing, moving his lips silently with the dialogue.)*

"Then, suddenly, Edward took a shuddering breath! Edward lived! The pressure of Christine's supple young breasts against his body had been enough to staunch the flow of blood, and with the innocence of youth, Christine did not realize that her kisses had been history's first incidence of mouth-to-mouth resuscitation!"

ANNOUNCER. You have been listening to an excerpt from *The Haunting of Christine*, the astonishingly successful first novel from author Juliano Montevideo. Only days after its release, this steamy bodice ripper has soared to the top of the best-seller lists, aided no doubt, by the controversy surrounding its origins. Who is Juliano Montevideo, or is this, as some suspect, merely the new pen name of convicted felon Carla Woods?

MAN. Close, but no cigar.

ANNOUNCER. The book's publishers remain resolutely silent. One fact remains certain: Whoever is cashing those royalty checks is undoubtedly laughing mysteriously, all the way to the bank! In our final entertainment segment this afternoon, we take you behind the scenes of the new documentary being filmed in...

> *(The **MAN** turns the sound off as we hear knocking on the front door. He opens the door, revealing **GRACE**, without briefcase, but with walking stick.)*

GRACE. Surprise!

MAN. Hi! I didn't expect you until tomorrow!

GRACE. Oh, if you're in the middle of something...

MAN. No, no, of course not! Come on in. Why didn't you call me? I would have picked you up...

GRACE. Thanks, but it's time I started managing things by myself. Driving is one of the things I can still do well.

> *(**GRACE** enters. She moves stiffly.)*

MAN. I know I keep saying it, but it's so great to see you walking again. Especially after that one doctor said you might never...

GRACE. God, it's strange coming back here. It seems like it all happened a long time ago.

MAN. It did. Almost a year. Can I fix you a drink?

> *(He presses a button on a small remote that he takes out of his pocket, and the bar pops out of the wall.)*

GRACE. No thanks. You get a kick out of this place, don't you.

MAN. *(Making the bar open and close.)* You know I do!

GRACE. I still can't believe that you bought it.

MAN. Yeah, well – what else am I going to do with all those royalty checks?

GRACE. *(Taking the remote out of his hand and placing it on a table.)* Buy a villa in Spain, a chateau on the Riviera… I just don't trust Carla's reasons for selling it to you.

MAN. She's gonna be locked up for the rest of her life for what she did to you – What's she going to do with it? Besides, you know I love this house. I love the theatricality of it, the whole funhouse thing.

GRACE. You know, I never did find out where all the pitfalls were…

MAN. Don't worry – I have! Give the house a chance, Grace. In a weird kind of way, it's what brought us together. *(He embraces her.)*

GRACE. It's all that time you spent beside my hospital bed that brought us together.

MAN. Maybe. But who cares? If you don't like this house, we'll buy a new one. Between your settlement and my royalties, we can live in Spain or the Riviera or on the moon if you want to!

*(***GRACE*** laughs.)*

The important thing is that it all turned out happily ever after. You're well on the road to recovery and I'm a best-selling author!

GRACE. About to star in the movie version of his own book!

MAN. Janet's story finally got told to the world, Carla Woods is safely and securely behind bars, and best of all – I finally managed to do something right and fall in love with a beautiful, wonderful lady.

GRACE. And I managed to fall in love with the tall, dark and handsome romantic hero who rescued me from the evil villainess!

MAN. Except heroes don't usually save the damsel by calling 9-1-1.

GRACE. Maybe you could work that into your next book.

MAN. Maybe...

GRACE. *(Picking up a glossy hardcover copy of* The Haunting of Christine *from the desk.)* I'm still surprised that Carla allowed you to claim authorship.

MAN. Why? You were the one who picked out the story cards that formed the plot, right? And Carla only wrote three paragraphs – I wrote the other two hundred and fifty-seven pages. If it belongs to anyone, it belongs to you and me, free and clear. But let's not waste time on that right now, okay? *(He takes her in his arms and kisses her.)*

GRACE. You know what? I think Carla was right all along.

MAN. *(Nibbling on her neck.)* Hhmnn?

GRACE. She said that if two people are meant to be together, then anything is possible. And if we're good and kind and patient enough, we can be like the romance heroines and live happily ever after.

MAN. Well, I don't know about happily ever after, but I have a great idea about how we could spend the next couple of hours...

GRACE. Oh?

MAN. How's the back feeling?

GRACE. Depends what you have in mind.

MAN. Here we are, all by ourselves in the middle of nowhere, no one to bother us for days and weeks and months...

GRACE. Whatever shall we do?!

MAN. *(As Edward.)* Surrender to your desires! Let me take you in my arms and sweep you into the eternal passion which lies in your soul!

GRACE. Oh, Edward!

> *(He lifts her in his arms, turns, and heads up the stairs.)*

MAN. Tonight, we will forget the world and all its troubles, and fall into an abyss of happiness, peace and contentment...

> *(The lights suddenly flicker, and strange noises are heard. The* **MAN** *sets* **GRACE** *carefully on her feet.)*

GRACE. Please tell me you've installed some new effects...?

MAN. Not me. I suddenly have this strange feeling that... Arghh!

> *(The stairs suddenly break open. Screaming, the* **MAN** *and* **GRACE** *drop through them and disappear.)*
>
> *(Blackout.)*